A Perfect Home for a Family

by

David L. Harrison

illustrated by

Roberta Angaramo

Holiday House / New York

For Jennifer—More!
—D. L. H.

For Dina and Bruno and their lovely house in the forest
—R. A.

Text copyright © 2013 by David L. Harrison
Illustrations copyright © 2013 by Roberta Angaramo
All Rights Reserved
HOLIDAY HOUSE is registered in the U.S. Patent and Trademark Office.
Printed and Bound in October 2012 at Toppan Leefung, DongGuan City, China.
The text typeface is Hank BT.
The artwork was created with acrylics.
www.holidayhouse.com
First Edition
1 3 5 7 9 10 8 6 4 2

Library of Congress Cataloging-in-Publication Data
Harrison, David L. (David Lee), 1937-
A perfect home for a family / by David L. Harrison ; illustrated by Roberta Angaramo. — 1st ed.
p. cm.
Summary: A family of raccoons searches for the perfect home, only to find
that what they had been looking for is right under their noses.
ISBN 978-0-8234-2338-5 (hardcover)
[1. Raccoons—Fiction. 2. Animals—Habitations—Fiction.] I. Angaramo, Roberta, ill. II. Title.
PZ7.H2474Pe 2012
[E]—dc22
2010039385

"What's that?" said Mama.

"What?" said Papa.

"That," said Mama.

"Oh no," said Papa.

"The Blue Jays have kids again.
We'll never get any sleep."

"This tree is noisy,"
said Mama.

"Crowded," said Papa,
"since the Opossums
moved upstairs."

"Follow me," said Mama.
"Where to?" said Papa.
"Town," said Mama.
"To someplace roomy
and quiet and peaceful.
The twins will be here soon."
"I'll find a real estate agent,"
said Papa.

"A. J. Squirrel at your service,"
said A. J. Squirrel.
"What do you have in mind?"
"Something roomy,"
said Papa.
"Quiet," said Mama.
"Peaceful," said Papa.

"You'll love
this sweet gum tree,"
said A. J.
Papa shook his head.
"Just another tree," he said.
"Small," said Mama.

"You'll adore
this garage,"
said A. J.
"Smells," said Papa.
"Car fumes,"
said Mama.

"You'll be crazy
about this attic,"
said A. J.
"Hmmm," said Mama.
"Roomy," said Papa.
"Quiet," said Mama.
"Peaceful," said Papa.

"How much?" said Mama.
"Ten acorns per month,"
said A. J.
"Eight," said Papa.
"Done," said A. J.

That night Mama dreamed about the twins.

Papa dreamed about acorns and berries.

But the next morning
something down below
made an awful noise.
It sounded like
WAAAAAAH!

"What's that?" said Mama.
"Don't know," said Papa.
"Some kind of critter
in our basement!"

"Oh no," said Mama.
"What can we do?"
"Stamp and stomp," said Papa.
Mama stamped.
Papa stomped.

They listened.
Something down below
made an awful noise.
It sounded like
YAP YAP YAP YAP
YAP YAP YAP YAP!

"What's that?" said Mama.
"Dog," said Papa.
"Can't stand dogs," said Mama.
"What can we do?"

"Hiss and snarl," said Papa.
Mama hissed.
Papa snarled.

They listened.
Something down below
made an awful noise.
It sounded like
WHAT'S THAT!?

"What's that?" said Mama.
"People," said Papa,
"right under our feet."
"I'm out of here," said Mama.

"How about that
sweet gum tree?"
said Papa.
"Don't like
that sweet gum tree,"
said Mama.

FOR RENT

"How about
the garage?"
said Papa.
"Don't like
the garage,"
said Mama.

"Where should we go?"
said Papa.
"I know," said Mama.
"Follow me."

"The Blue Jays moved," said Papa.
"The Opossums moved too," said Mama.
"Roomy," said Papa.
"Quiet," said Mama.
"Peaceful," said Papa.

"No place like home,"
said Mama.
"I agree," said Papa.

That very night,
in a perfect place,
the twins were born.